ALSO BY ROB DAVIDSON

FICTION
*The Farther Shore*
*Field Observations*

CRITICISM
*The Master and the Dean: The Literary Criticism
of Henry James and William Dean Howells*

# SPECTATORS

# SPECTATORS

Flash Fictions by
Rob Davidson

Five Oaks Press
FIVE-OAKS-PRESS.COM

ISBN: 978-1-944355-31-9


Five Oaks Press
Newburgh, NY 12550
five-oaks-press.com
editor@five-oaks-press.com


Cover Art: Tom Patton, *Man Videotaping the Grand Canyon, Arizona, 2010* from *The Spectacle of Ordinary Spectators*

Author photo credit: Linda Rogers

Interior and Cover Design: Lynn Houston

Printed in the U.S.A.

## ACKNOWLEDGMENTS

Some of these fictions first appeared in the following literary journals, sometimes in different form:

*Along These Lines*: "Walter: Six Meditations"
*Apricrot Blossom*: "Hey, Pumpkinhead"
*Arroyo Literary Review*: "Virginia Steps into Her Stream" and "What Henry Said"
*Roger: An Art and Literary Magazine*: "Author's Note"
*Saranac Review*: "Women Going Opposite Ways" and "Hoover Dam"
*South Dakota Review*: "The Mistake of Waiting," "The Price of the Journey," and "Sky Glider"

In addition, "Hoover Dam" was reprinted in *re: home* (1078 Gallery, Chico, CA, 2012) and an earlier version of "Walter: Six Meditations" appeared in *Fog & Woodsmoke: Behind the Image* (Ed. Stephani Schaefer. Duluth, MN: Lost Hills Books, 2011).

Many of these flash fictions were inspired by the work of photographers and visual artists: Tom Patton, Stephani Schaefer, and Sara Umemoto. Their excellent work stirred the muse in new ways, and I owe them each a debt of gratitude. Thanks to Sarah Pape, who paired me with Tom Patton for an image-and-text collaboration at the 1078 Gallery in Chico, California in 2012, the genesis moment for much of this book.

A number of these fictions were exhibited alongside Tom Patton's photographs at the Morris Graves Museum of Art in Eureka, California, December 2016-January 2017.

The epigraph for "The Price of the Journey" is taken from the poem "Written on the Wall at Xilin Temple," by Su Dongpo. Translated by Beata Grant. (*Zen Poems*. Ed. Peter Harris. New York: Everyman-Knopf, 1999.)

The final line of "Tree Line" is modified from the final line of "Ten Bulls: The Zen Ox-Herding Pictures," by Kakuan. Translated by Nyogen Senzaki and Paul Reps. (*Entering the Stream: An Introduction to The Buddha and His Teachings.* Ed. Samuel Bercholz and Sherab Chödzin Kohn. Boston: Shambhala, 1993.)

The final line of "The Best View" is paraphrased from Raymond Carver's poem "Drinking While Driving." (*All of Us: The Collected Poems.* New York: Knopf, 1998.)

The final line of "This Story That You're Reading" is lovingly borrowed from the William Stafford poem "You Reading This, Be Ready." (*The Way It Is: New & Selected Poems.* St. Paul, MN: Graywolf, 1999.)

# CONTENTS

III. Fog & Woodsmoke

*for Linda*

# I. Spectators

## CLEAN PILGRIM
### Vernal Falls, Yosemite

He stands before the world, clean pilgrim in search of a song. It is the rushing roar of the falls, one final note droning into eternity. Drop after rushing drop chisels its demands into stone, a lasting record of compulsion and desire. Sing of the banker's greed, and the pornographer's heart-empty lust! Sing of a child's hunger for knowledge, and a pilgrim's blind aspiration! For that which one cannot help but do becomes that which one must do.

Water shapes our lives. Water is the ceaseless murmur of language, an inky stream beckoning all to begin again.

A pilgrim stands before you, humble and alone, surrounded by a chorus of water. When he sings, please bend to listen.

## HOOVER DAM

He emerges from the concrete belly of the dam, that black, humid pit, into blinding sunlight. He removes his hard hat, checks his messages. Thumb dances on keyboard, rapidly entering characters. There is no one to talk to about any of this—the pressure he feels pushing down on him, the futility of pushing back. Deep inside, he feels the ancient turbines turn. He feels the bristling energy, freely shares it with a wife and three children. But there are cracks in his foundation. Perhaps it's inevitable: every dam must fail. Because look what it's up against. Water always wins. It just keeps coming, flowing down the canyon, steady and relentless.

Many years ago he built a wall, made it as thick as he could. But anything can be worn down with time. Now he feels it—the dampness seeping in, eroding his foundation. There was a day, not long ago, when the first chunk crumbled off; now it's a small hole. Water works that scar, soaking and lapping, licking and stroking, probing with its wet tongue. He presses send, texting himself: *Now is the end of the beginning of the end.*

## THE PRICE OF THE JOURNEY

*If the true face of Mount Lu*
*cannot be known,*
*It is because the one looking at it*
*is standing in its midst.*
—Su Dongpo

Knowledge arrives, thirsty and talking too much. What can we do but stare, mouth open, in naked wonder. Knowledge babbles in chumbling tongue, strange language we've never heard, spouting tales mysterious and incomprehensible. Why trust it? Why listen?

Ours is a form of desire, the hope that we too may one day travel to distant lands. We crave a map, but knowledge burns all maps. Its journey is blind, grasping, a desperate push beyond all limits.

Every moment we linger in not-knowing, every moment we accept incomprehension, we travel farther. We stand at a crossroads, unsure of which fork to follow. We stare, we gape, we dream and draw, drunk with misdirection. Not lost, we are eternally arriving.

# THE BEST VIEW

Having picked up the camera, she cannot put it down. She prefers to view the world as she has made it, a gentle prison of frame and perspective. Each picture is an improvement, for the world is a messy place.

Yet her images do not behave themselves. Like children, they grow their own lives. Each means what it wants to mean, or what the viewer says it means. Perhaps an artist is nothing more than a parent learning to let go, releasing images into a disorderly world.

Perhaps there shall emerge one true picture, an image so strong none can doubt it. Having seen it, all will believe, all will accept its truth—her truth, the world she has made.

Her finger is warm, the red button so smooth, so easy to press. Any moment now, something will happen.

## THE STORIES WE TELL OURSELVES
Grand Canyon

*Nature likes to hide itself.*
—Heraclitus

He will not remember the canyon. He will not remember the smell of sage, or the breeze, just slightly cool, wafting up from the riverbed. He will not remember hawks soaring on thermals, hovering like terrible angels. He will not remember a lizard perched nearby, watching with a solemn black eye.

He will remember taking multiple shots from different angles; he will remember adjusting for light and resolution, each decision so fascinatingly different. He shoots again and again, and with each new image he builds another, different canyon, thereby justifying the existence of the first.

We are only the stories we tell ourselves.

## ODE TO A SELFIE

It is not Windsor Castle but herself in front of Windsor Castle that she records. For she fears above all things the erasure of memory, the inability to recall events, places, people. She fears oblivion and losing every moment of her life, each gesture and decision, each word. She wishes to carry these things forward, storing them away in the hope that what she leaves behind might one day mean something, somewhere, to someone. She cannot bear to think of the alternative, though it governs her every gesture.

## SEARCHING FOR MONUMENTS
### Monument Valley, Utah

Men search for monuments, they debate and confirm, slowly building a story, at once the record of their search and the very spectacle they seek. On their wet, rough tongues shall be built an empire, one of roadways carved from rock, sculpted slabs licked clean by God's weary tongue.

The world stands before us in need of language, a site on which we build our stories, making meaning. Nature without its narrative is nothing but a child's dream of shapes and colors.

## NATURE: TALKING POINTS
### Niagara Falls

What is Nature, and what is Wal-Mart? The only wild thing here is that guy's outfit.

The true point of Nature is to remind us of everything we've built to hide it. Guardrails only protect us from ourselves. We love limits; we feel safer behind an enforced perspective. Decisions have been made for us in advance: the best photo angles thoughtfully suggested on low-set signs; the story of each landscape spelled out on placards; a map with numbered highlights. To be in Nature is to follow orders.

## WOMAN WITH NO HANDS

A woman with no hands, lost in an absurd, oversized jacket, steps timidly. Always a little behind, she follows others, waits for commands. She fears everything: dirt, sun, germs, air. She moved into her daughter's home eighteen months ago, a planned retreat. She spends her days at the kitchen table sipping tea, nibbling toast, listening to the radio. Her daughter takes her places, says they must get out. To the store or the park. It is this woman's duty to obey, she who once commanded all respect. Daughter steps forward boldly, leading; mother follows. With no hands there is nothing to grasp, nothing to hold, like the Buddha said.

## WHAT THE CANYON KNOWS
Grand Canyon


The cupped hand of the canyon holds the river so gently. How, when water can only erode it?

He, too, cradles a wound—something so deep it defines him. He's always tried to hide it, spinning his beautiful lies, but maybe this canyon is right. Maybe the best thing to do is to reveal it: layered and complex, forever shifting and reshaping. Only then will others truly know him; only then will he know himself.

But where would he begin? What are the actor's first lines?

Turning his back on the problem, he shuffles up the stairs, returning to a familiar role. Cast in a scene already unfolding, he knows his lines by heart, and fondly. The lies of others are never as sweet as the lies we tell ourselves.

## A BOY WHO TALKS TO RIVERS

He is a boy who talks to rivers, issuing orders and proclamations, sharing secrets and desires. The river burbles on, accepting every word as it goes about its watery business. The rocks and stones, so hard and slow to change, can afford indifference. The trees alone bend to listen, ever patient.

Screaming himself hoarse, the boy hasn't yet learned to give audience. The rocks, in their stony silence, speak. In turning their green ears to listen, the trees offer a teaching. And that perky river, wending its way in partner with its neighbors, palavers too.

There is inside us a child's wish that the world would yield to our demands. Yet it's only when we stop to listen that something unexpected opens, like the ear of a parenthesis.

## THE VIRTUE OF WAITING

A professor barks into a bullhorn; students are camped out on the president's lawn; a girl hands out flyers. The reporter lowers her camera. None of it is news, not yet.

Patience is an old friend, often rewarded.

Something sleeps in all of us, an ancient beast waiting to stir. At any moment it might rise up and roar, and when it does you want a camera there because that is your moment, your golden chance, perhaps the only time in your life you'll do something worthy of having the world watch. The news is not a picture of who we are; it is a drunken god's dream, who we wish we were.

## TREE LINE
Mount Shasta


He crosses the tree line, searching for a clearer view. It's nothing like he imagined: a cold wind batters and bites him; tiny, desperate shrubs cling to the earth. He stands exposed, wearing the colors of the barren rock face, a borrowed sense of hardness. Here, his desires seem foreign and useless, like the currency of a lost civilization.

Below him, a green line of trees: white firs, limbs flung open like a mother's arms. The smell of a campfire, the clatter of dishware, the chatter of children—everything he thought he'd left behind.

The wind whispers, *We are not who we think we are. We are not who we think we are.*

Yield, gain, loss—what of it? Sing, pilgrim, returned from a dry country. Now, before you, the dead trees become alive.

## THE TOURIST

The tourist stands always at one remove, just out of reach. The tourist has the luxury of stepping away while you must putter and pose, going about your Wednesday morning, which is like every Wednesday morning everywhere: universally slow. Your spirit drags as you catalog your miseries, which you're good at collecting. You have so many.

The tourist gets to say, I am interested in you but only in a small kind of way. What else is there around here? The tourist gets to walk away, never to return. And you get to hate him for it.

Of course, the tourist eventually arrives home and soon enough his own miseries arise, but then he's not a tourist anymore, just a traveler returned, a fellow sufferer worthy of compassion. It's perfectly sensible, like an egg.

## SKY GLIDER
### Above the Santa Cruz Boardwalk

Sky Glider floats above the crowd, hovers over and above the crowd, a spectacle to behold. Behold a dream of elevation, behold a dream of escape. Escape all attention, dispense no favors, judge none other than one's self. Self-interested and sublime, Sky Glider is a perfect fiction, a willing, milling million people's dream. Dream of purpose, dream of goals, dream a reason to be. Be in this world, having created it. It appears there's nothing to do but ride around this world in circles, ignoring countless pleas for intervention (he is indifferent), for a miracle (he is powerless), for hope (he is hopeless). Helpless is Sky Glider, hovering above this world of goals and outcomes, predictions and rewards. Reword the litany of the log flume, chant down the ceremony of the Tilt-a-Whirl, upend the blessing of the bumper cars. Cars he rides in endless circles, first this way, then that. That he hovers above the milling millions he created means nothing. Nothing, but why? Why, asks he who hates the world he created because he is not, can never be, part of it. It pains him to wonder who made him, why they took the trouble to make Sky Glider.

## CHARLEMAGNE AT POINT ZERO
### Cathédrale de Notre-Dame de Paris

Charlemagne, Pater Europæ, sits astride his steed, noble servants at his side. He raises his scepter, forever unifying and defining a continent, forever advancing his Christian cause, forever brutalizing the infidels and the quarrelsome.

Every story has its Point Zero: genesis of empire, point from which all measurements are drawn. Fear not, O King. Your story survives. The very Republic in which we stand is a byproduct of your gesture. Not that it looks like it. In your presence people mill about, strolling here and there, checking messages and consulting maps. Some are hungry, some are horny, some don't know what time it is. This is the true and final consequence of empire: to be lost in the quotidian, the everyday, the banal.

Forever shall you sit, Charlemagne, tarnished and ignored. Yes, you rule us, fine.

## INVISIBLE RIVER

Citizens occupy towers of tinted windows, overlooking plazas of pale grass. With binoculars pressed to eye sockets, they record notes, send updates. Ten thousand cameras scan city sidewalks, streets and alleys. Our goal is to leave nothing unseen.

What we find is always the same: pilgrims strolling aimlessly, ignoring pathways, dropping coats and bags. In this era, it is dangerous to own things. Better to be anonymous, in possession of nothing, to blend in and get to work, for ours is a city of data, that invisible river we call information.

You have come to us, O pilgrim, wanderer of the ways. You undertook a journey in search of knowledge. Now your journey is complete: you have been recorded and cross-checked, indexed and approved. You are knowledge, our knowledge. And now you shall enter the stream, feel the tug of a current so strong there can be only one response.

Citizen, put down your lendings; you need nothing here. Our sacred responsibility is now yours. Even as we speak new pilgrims arrive, wandering from points afar. Thus the city of knowledge grows. Choose a tower and move toward it. It is time.

## SPECTATORS

Behold the growing congregation, the swelling throng. We are gathered here today in confusion, clutching guide books and maps, rail tickets and a street address for a café that someone assured us is the best place to get lunch. We are never very sure what we're looking at; you can tell us but we won't remember. We'll take a photo anyway, shoot a video. We are restless, always moving on, never staying in one place for long. To your crumbling empires and wasted civilizations we flock. You hate us, yet obey our requests, for we have disposable income and an urge to buy.

We are tourists; we are spectators.

We stand before you, a roaming band and a special breed: enchanted or distracted, aware or insensate, we exist both to observe and to be observed, for wherever we go we present ourselves, a living spectacle, a strange circle at once sublime and absurd. We ask only that you acknowledge, as you read this, that you have joined us. Welcome.

## II. Signals & Marches

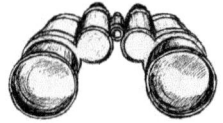

## THE MISTAKE OF WAITING

The mistake most commonly made by those asked to wait is to focus on that which has not yet happened. The anticipation of action, the expectation of the event, the anxiety of delay: these obscure the truth of waiting, which is a radiant stasis.

He knows what he's waiting for. He knows it's coming, sooner or later. He just doesn't know exactly when, or how, or what happens next. These are the things he thinks about, but that is precisely his mistake: to focus on a mysterious future—a thing at once terrifying and banal—and not on the wait itself.

He will be waiting for a good while yet. He ought to turn his attention accordingly.

There is only the waiting itself, for which there is no wait. The truth of waiting is that one should endeavor to do only that, without expectation or desire. Accept this bright parade of moments; it is your story now.

## IN THE CITY OF YOUTH

In the city of youth traffic moves in one direction, guided by arrows and signs; lights are green, but the streets are empty.

In the city of youth all distances are vast; there's always far to go, and never a precise destination.

In the city of youth all routes are tentative; one waits and waits for transport: the waiting is endless.

In the city of youth adults are distant, unreachable; they speak a strange language.

In the city of youth maps are inscrutable, a tangled mess of lines and shapes; every name sounds funny.

In the city of youth there are gates and fences, locked doors and windows; only buildings stand tall, reaching ever higher, their heads wrapped in billowy clouds.

## WOMEN GOING OPPOSITE WAYS

*The path up and down
is one and the same.*
—Heraclitus

One sister remembers white paper lanterns dangling from string. Soft music and candles. A mother's smile. It was like that once, she says. Even you can't deny it.

The other sister remembers shouting, slammed doors, plates shattered against walls. Father weeping into his hands, the dirt around his eyes running like mascara. How can you forget, she says. How dare you.

There is no path. Sisters spill out into the wilderness. Different directions toward a shared goal: make the journey mean something.

## GIRL WITH APPLE

Walking towards Victoria Tower, she turns to ask what he meant by that, but he's gone, lost in the crowd of St. Margaret Street. The remains of an apple rest between finger and thumb. Another thing shared freely, another thing he sank his teeth into, another small mess in her hand. Meat spent, gnawed to the core. Something to toss.

She stands before Parliament, house of laws and decisions. She knows he'll never return. Her bag, half-full like her heart: a cavity aching to be filled. She is the girl in shoes with no laces, unprepared for her journey. Turn, she tells herself, turn and begin.

# WHAT IS LOST

His stride speaks: he knows his direction, his destination never in doubt. He knows his place, subject to Queen and Empire. City streets are bounded by fences. Signs mark every corner. It is very hard to be lost.

Across the street scaffolding covers a new building, something going up, something in the process of becoming. Something he doesn't yet control.

There is a cry, and a loud crash. Heads turn.

Something spirals up from his memory—thin taper of smoke, a fire he long thought extinguished. It is *his* cry, *his* crack-up: something ravaged long ago. Dirty fingers tickle his throat; a dry tongue whispers an ancient name.

If he pauses even for a moment to consider it, he'll miss a step, or worse. He must not break his stride; he must move on. There is nothing in this world without its price, however carefully hidden.

## HOW TO HURT THEM

You hurt them with your lies. You hurt them with your indifference. You hurt them with your insincerity, your plastic affirmations. You hurt them when you forget. You hurt them when you remember. You hurt them when you least expect it. You hurt them without trying. When you hurt them, you tell yourself it's an accident, an aberration, a one-time thing. But you hurt them so often you wonder if it isn't in your nature to hurt them.

You want to hurt them. You need to hurt them. Because when you do you feel a strange power: a dark, shadowed wing unfolds.

This is how you hurt them. This is why you hurt them. And this is why, though you've told yourself a thousand times to stop, you won't.

You want to get better, and you will.

## WOMAN ANNOYED

Not that one again. Don't you know it never works? I don't know why you keep asking. You're so relentless. You're so obsessed. You think everyone will come around to see things your way, but you're wrong. I know what you're on about. I see through your lies, your dissembling. Because you're so obvious. Because it's always the same thing. You only want one thing, though you ask a thousand ways.

Let me tell you something: you're not growing stronger, you're growing weaker, more child-like. That's what you are now. You're a child with your wants and needs, your desire to have things your way. You want someone to cater to you. You want someone to clean up your mess. You want someone to tell you it's all right. But it's not all right, not with me it's not. I know you. I'm not stupid. And I'm not having it, not for one single second.

## THE PRISONER

He stands in shadows, half-lit. He stands at corners, half-hidden. Thus he breaks his master's gaze, resists control. Sedition comes in small gestures, bound always to the iron chain of fealty.

He waits at his master's door, ever dutiful, ever willing. He listens, he watches, learning the ways of his master—his language, his movements. Thus he plans his future, his freedom, his revenge. Every thief is first a clever mimic.

He views imprisonment as a gift, an opportunity. It is a kind of courage, this patience. Thus he imagines another self, a new history told in a new language. There is no revolution without an order to overthrow.

## TESTIMONY

When he finds me he says nothing. Just perches on a little green fence and lights a cigarette. Watching me. Waiting me out. We both know I won't run. When they find you, it's over. What is Paris but a maze? God's sewer.

Then he makes the call. He speaks quietly, gaze unbroken. Now it's certain. In a few minutes a red van will arrive. The side door will open. A hand will beckon. And it will start all over again, the same as before. I will be who they want me to be, say the words they long to hear, dress in their uniform and dance to their music, so plastic and thin.

I don't know why you listen; my testament can only be false. You know this as well as anyone, yet you adore me.

## VIRGINIA STEPS INTO HER STREAM

Virginia steps into her stream only to find another road, its stones a glossy ribbon moving downstream. The direction of water always so sure. She walks under water, the shorelines blurry with autumn's auburn brush. The important thing, always, is to look good when you're drowning.

A snail, late of Kew Gardens, turns away, glued to his stick. Blithely slurping, the invertebrate he's always been. You can't really blame him: slobbering along in a daze, leaving his sticky trail. He carries that absurd shell, history of burdens unshakeable, whorling up to its one, fine point. To remove it—not that he ever would—would expose him for what he is: naked, writhing, glistening in his own juices.

Virginia, carried by other currents, turns her back on him.

## LOOK GOOD DEAD

Strange woman, dreaming of a fallen father. Dirt taster, lover of grass, student of worms. A finger probes after moles, blind and afraid. Darkness surrounds them even in brightest daylight.

Gravity, a caress best felt across the body.

If she sleeps, let her sleep. It is the dream of every woman to look good dead.

# FAILURE

Palm fronds clack like ancient accusations, hovering out of reach. They grow and thrive, shading others even as he burns in the sun.

The slap of flesh on a volleyball; a body falls. The opponent waits, hands on hips, eyes narrow.

We don't think of failure in this way: a sunny day along the coast, the air just slightly cool. Memory grabs at our lives, like a losing player's fingers thrust into the sand. We throw it all to the wind, praying it won't spit back.

# HEY, PUMPKINHEAD

This is what passes for achievement: to climb that staircase through the clouds, chest heaving, breath rapid and hot, only to find no final destination. Just the next point of departure.

Those who came before you were all alike: slowly ripening, waiting until someone cut them free. They float away in like manner, magisterially, waiting for a gust of wind to blow them here or there.

Not you. You're of a different kind. You cut your own stem years ago, felt the ripening agents earlier than most. You walk around with your tough skin and your multiple piercings and you *know* your hardness runs deep, way below the collar. But you didn't know how deep. You didn't know that such toughness binds you in place, rooting you in a different way, leaving you unable to fly.

## THE MELODY OF EXPECTATION

The man says nothing is going to happen, nothing *ever* happens. Tomorrow will be the same as today and yesterday. His road runs in a fixed line, hitting a wall on the other side of a plaza, dressed in faded graffiti. The sloganeers are long gone, facing cleaner, brighter walls.

The boy says anything might be out there, you never know. He waits hopefully, with the patience of one who has seen very little but trusts the world exists to open before him in splendor. His eyes follow the gentle curve of a new road, bowing to the horizon.

There is inside of us dark music, the melody of expectation.

## WAITING FOR A SIGNAL

As her friend leaves, the woman in the red suit turns to face the distances of the afternoon. Her friend is getting married again. Her friend is happy. She wants to be happy for her friend, but she thinks only of her own failed marriage. There was a short, good time followed by a longer, miserable time. Then came the hard words, impossible to retract or erase. Then came the thousand nights alone, the silences of an empty house. Leftovers eaten at a late hour, the television murmuring in the corner. Then came the fear.

On her street corner, the light is slow to change. Why is she always the one to wait? She could cross the street now. There is no traffic, no danger. Also no direction, no reason to move. The state of her heart: a lawless conspiracy.

## THE CREWMAN'S DREAM

Engines roaring, she lumbers along the airstrip like an old bear. She lifts her nose, front wheels dangling from her chin. Tail low, almost scraping the ground, she lifts off and for just a moment she's hovering, making her mind up about which way she's going to go, up or down. Then one wing dips and the other rises, and she's gone in a sonorous, rushing roar.

I like her best when she's at rest, so quiet and still. This great gray beast with her cargo doors open, beckoning me to crawl inside, to be strapped to her ribs, to have those doors close me in. To be washed in the deafening roar of engines, baptism of flight.

This is my dream: together we touch down in a new town. Her doors open and I walk out into sunshine and smiles. A girl waves to me from a new Corvette. She knows my name and where we're going. And I'm right on time.

## THE REVOLUTION BEGINS

Let there always be some guy with a bullhorn and a screed. Let there always be the agitator and his polemic, enumerating dull points in leaden language. Let there always be a space for his kind, however narrow: perched on the corner of a raised flowerbed, for instance, shouting at students as they stumble off to a lecture.

This guy is into something.

This guy is telling it like it is.

This guy knows.

The revolution begins at ten o'clock of a Tuesday morning.

## TODAY'S LESSON

A sunny Thursday afternoon, the spring heat just rising, faint smell of lilac on the breeze. Collar open, tie stuffed in pocket—no need of that now. Across town a warehouse stands half-empty, anticipating orders. A district manager awaits a call to confirm. A wife mutters prayers as she weeds another flowerbed. A son boasts that his dad's best at everything.

What are the expectations of others?

A leaf blows on a tree, gently rocking the bough. Each leaf is destined to fall. Yet the tree stands firmly rooted, unshaken.

Perhaps a slow walk along The Mall to Trafalgar Square, then Charing Cross. Perhaps a pint with the boys back at the Old Crow and Eagle, a laugh over the day's headlines, the state of things—what else can you do? Disappointment has its benefits, nudging us toward joy.

# HAROLD'S DREAM: SUITE IN FOUR PANES

In one, Harold dreams of a saint standing, head bowed and hands folded, patiently awaiting martyrdom. Fireballs glow at his feet; the end is near, his finest hour.

In another, Harold dreams of a window in the crenellated corner of a big house. There lives an ancient spinster, silent to the world outside, considered odd. Yet she is prey to nothing. She controls her world, the pages of her heart burning with a love untouched, untrammeled, undiminished. Such is the empire of her mind.

And Harold dreams of the house below that room, separated by a rupture so ancient it has no name. The house's windows never open; the air inside is musty and stale. Outside, the world has moved on, filled with stoplights, bus signs, and travelers indifferent to ancient tales.

But not Harold: he dreams of a stone tower, elegantly carved, decorated with heraldic shields, a world filled with words like duty, obligation, and honor, which waft before him now like candle smoke, disappearing into air.

# III. Fog & Woodsmoke

# WALTER: SIX MEDITATIONS

## 1. Blackbirds at Dusk

First, there are the birds Walter doesn't see: thoughts that leap off the branch, take wing, and are gone—the lightest of feelings. The birds he sees are memories not yet ready for flight, weighing down his branches.

Josephine, a girl he knows. Knew. He wants to write her story, to write of a night they sat in the corner of a bar for hours, her breath on his cheek, all lime-soaked and fucked up. She wanted him to say something. He couldn't say it, his tongue twisted in a knot. Last call: the bartender raised the lights. In the glare, Josephine narrowed her eyes. She left him with a table of empties.

In the story he wants to write, the lovers stand on the pavement outside as drinkers stumble like raindrops into the night. Smoke crawls up the side of her cheek. They move toward each other slowly. His nose brushes her ear; her breast is soft against his arm. In the story he wants to write, the man understands that this woman is a bird delicately poised for flight, already a wing unfolded. He speaks. He has things to say, words that indicate he is sensitive, aware, but not overly sentimental. Such qualities make him desirable. If a story is a power struggle, a little war between desire and fear, between him and her, the man wins. But Walter hasn't yet written this story.

One bird flew, and one remained. Failure, sharp as a beak.

## 2. Flooded Road

Road meets water. As usual, Walter lacks the thing he needs: a boat. Suddenly, it is the solution to many problems; if he had a boat, he might move freely on vast waters, navigating streams and rivers, crossing lakes and inland seas. If he had a boat, he'd transgress borders, ignoring petty geography and its attempts to shape his life. Everyone knows water shapes land! If he had a boat, he'd be its captain, the admiral of his own fleet. If he had a boat, he could trace all that water back to its source, that mysterious, burbling black spring: the fountainhead of many defeats, many lost years on dry land. He'd leap from his boat into that water, swimming down, down, down to the bottom, where he'd place his mouth over the gushing orifice, gorging himself. If he could, he'd swallow every last drop, draining the world of something, but of course one can never be certain what that might mean. One man's miracle is another's catastrophe.

## 3. Roadside Marker

A roadside marker, thinks Walter, is an exercise in revisionist history, an *écriture* of the heart. It's an attempt to say something to others that, no doubt, was misunderstood or unheard while the deceased was alive. Words, gestures, gifts left not for the dead, but for the living: to reassure them that they did what they were supposed to have done, that they loved as much as they could, that they cherished and valued and complimented the beloved when—and Walter knows this—the guy who drove his Ford into that tree last March was actually a real son of a bitch.

Walter's monument, should he build one, would not look backward; there stands a litany of failure and despair, lost opportunities and half-realized goals. Walter's monument would be to the future, to the lives and possibilities still unborn and becoming, to the potential surrounding us, to the alternatives we can't yet embrace, the decisions we haven't yet the courage to make, the adventures we dream of and promise we'll attend to tomorrow. The idealized future is every ounce the lie that is the idealized past, but with one difference: there is that tender slice of possibility, the promise of *what if*, the knowledge that, with the next turn, the next blank page, the next girl you meet, your life might change.

Walter waits for something to happen, for when that something happens the past will be rewritten to anticipate what it couldn't have foretold—which is chance, really—sanctifying the present by making it inevitable.

## 4. Flyway

This flight of birds, an open parenthesis moving through the sky (signifying additional context or supplementary information not otherwise directly relevant to the main clause. Many readers skip parenthetical statements, assuming that the information is somehow "optional," or of lesser value. Yet Walter often finds the best information in parentheses—witty asides and tangential digressions on open display, as it were, in the middle of a sentence, where any reader can see it, not lurking about in the cellar like a footnote.[1] Yet, does not an open parenthesis demand a companion? Without it, the reader becomes lost, searching in vain for the absent partner), demanding closure.

[1] Where people tuck away the useless stuff—arcane scholarly digressions, long-winded bibliographic asides, quarrels over textual authority. How many people read footnotes? How many read beyond a line or two? Persistent readers are occasionally rewarded. They might find, for instance, a buried confession, such as the one Walter would like to proffer now to his beloved Josephine, muse incomprehensible. Her smile is missed. So is her slender wrist, around which he wrapped thumb and middle finger, touching their tips and feeling, in the soft flesh of his fingertip, her rapid, thrumming pulse. She liked him to do this as they made love, her fantasy of being bound—however gently—an added thrill as he hovered over her, gazing into her eyes. Walter has had much time to mull over such ironies, to catalog and cross-reference them, one by one. He has become a librarian of his own heart, assigning each memory its call number and subject heading: Defeat, minor. Defeat, major. Time, happy (see also *fleeting*). Opportunity, missed.

## 5. Fog and Woodsmoke

In this town, you can stand in the middle of the street for hours and no one will hit you, no matter how badly you want it.

December, five a.m. The air smells of woodsmoke and diesel exhaust. Walter longs for snow; he imagines the first flake falling, tumbling in the air, its tines like frail hands. But it rarely snows in this valley, where in winter the almond trees are skeletal and bare, even as the ground sprouts a blanket of emerald green grass. Fog covers everything in vague suggestion.

Soon he will return to his small cottage nestled beside the orchards. He'll toss another log into the woodstove, pour a cup of coffee, and sit down at his desk to do the only thing left to do. There are pages to be filled, words to be written, an empire of language waiting to rise. There is a Josephine waiting to be constructed: one who listens, loves, forgives. Walter serves her, humbly offering up a thousand words a day.

In a corner of his cottage sit his publications: a modest stack of chapbooks, journals, books. Walter shores these fragments against his ruins, etc., for it is this that gives shape to his existence, and purpose to his days. The world without words is the world unmade; it is not life that gives shape to art, but art that gives shape to life.

## 6. Pavement Ends

All pavement ends somewhere. Walter knows he's running out of road. He needs to make a turn, double back on himself, move in another direction. Or simply to stop. He keeps moving when stillness is the only sensible option, but then he's never been good at sitting still and just becoming. Each moment the perfect image of itself: that's not what Walter wants. He wants motion, the illusion of progress. Stasis kills the heart. If a mountain sat before him, he'd climb the mountain. A cloud of fog, he'd enter it. He's in it now. Has been for years. Coming or going? Walter rarely knows.

## THIS IS THE STORY

So, I'm reading this book and I get an idea. I reach for my pencil and start to jot down the idea, thinking as I write that this is a good idea, one I'll want to remember later. As I'm writing that first idea a second idea occurs to me, even better than the first. But I can't stop writing the first idea because I'm in the middle of it. I finish writing the first idea and I leave a long em dash—

I pause to think of the second idea, but it's gone. I wait. I look out the window at the peonies, blooming now in my yard. A bird chirps merrily in a tree. The second idea, the one I thought was so good, is gone, irretrievable. Maybe it will return, maybe it won't. Maybe it isn't a problem at all. Maybe it's the nature of one thought to find its way to paper, and for another to vanish, lost in the maze of neurons and misfiring synapses, prompting me out of my chair and to my desk. No accident at all, this is the story.

## WHAT HENRY SAID

He said if you want to be an artist you have to learn to *look*. He said press your face close, into the space provided. He said look through the opening you're given, record what *you* see. So, all right, it's no house of fiction, no grand mansion of a hundred windows. That was *his* damn house. Yours isn't like that at all. It's not even a house—more like a hut, slapped together out of cheap pine panels. And you don't have a window, just some crazy pattern cut by a madman with a jig saw, its edges rough and unsanded. Turns out the shape of that hole determines what you can see—a square window shows you a square world.

What if your window is a girl? Then all your life you see not a world, but a world through a girl.

Press yourself to it, darling. *Look*. Let those rough edges bite into your flesh. If you bleed a little, it's all right. *Look*.

# THIS STORY THAT YOU'RE READING

This story that you're reading is slow to awaken. It's checked out, it's got its earbuds in, it's catching forty winks in the corner. Maybe it had too much to drink last night. Maybe it stayed up late, talking. This story likes the sound of its own voice.

Some of its fellow stories complain that that's all it is: voice and no content. No meat. Bring back the days of Dreiser, they say, the savage prolixity of Norris, the foot-on-the-bar politics of Steinbeck. Give us Henry James and long sentences filled with velvety turns. Give us something more than that windbag of the first-person declarative, obsessing over objects and opinions.

This story wants to keep it real. This story wears a hoodie and jeans. This story is chill. But don't let that fool you. This story is ambitious, crazy ambitious. This story is an early draft, in a state of becoming. The next time you read this story it will be different—new clothes, new haircut, new music.

This story is on its way, but it's only partway there. This story is on a layover, between flights, behind schedule. Give it a little time. This story will make itself heard, will make you want to listen. You, reading this, be ready.

## AUTHOR'S NOTE

My name is Rob. I work for Davidson.

It is I, Rob, who has a wife and two children. I mow my lawn, vote my conscience, wave to the neighbors. If there are a few hard-earned dollars in my bank account, it is because I work: I spend roughly four hundred hours each year in a classroom or a lecture hall, standing before students and colleagues talking about what he, Davidson, does. I speak his language, one of drafting and revision, artifice and craft, form and content. I do this willingly, lovingly, without an ounce of resentment. All for Davidson.

He couldn't live for five minutes without me, his Rob.

Davidson lives just two hours a day. Longer in summer, or during winter breaks. He might resurrect himself for four, five hours a day then. But during the school year, when I have my son's soiled diaper in one hand and a student essay in the other and the phone is ringing, he's damn lucky to get his two hours, believe me. He's greedy, you see. If you overlook him, ignore him, try to forget about him, he'll be right there, at my throat, scratching and pleading and making his incessant, ultimately unstoppable demands. And so I re-arrange my life to accommodate him. I make and cancel plans. I schedule my trips to the grocery, to the playground, to the post office around his two hours. I teach my classes and earn my paycheck so that he, Davidson, may live.

Occasionally, I am invited to read his work before some group or other. A few people might line up afterwards to buy a book and to ask questions. They want, of course, to speak with him. I cannot muster the courage to tell them he didn't come. He's never, ever available for this kind of public appearance. No one can ever see him or visit or ask him a question. He shall never respond.

He lives, you see, a strange kind of existence, hidden away in that room of his. Tapping away on his keyboard, constructing his city of language. (No, not city. Sorry, Davidson, but you haven't yet written your city. Not even a town. A village, perhaps. A hamlet.) It is there he lives, issuing all-too-infrequently his latest missive, a small bundle of white paper with neat, blank ink. Printing. Words.

He's most proud of that. Only that, I suppose, for that is all he is: a wordsmith, a kind of artisan or craftsman. That is the one thing, the only thing, he does. Me, I'm not exactly proud of him. Grateful, in a way. Oddly enough, it is what he does that allows me to do what I do. Teaching allows me to pay the mortgage on my house, to buy my kids a new shirt or a book, to take the wife out for dinner and a movie now and again. Teaching allows me to live my ordinary, quiet life on my ordinary, quiet cul-de-sac in this ordinary, quiet town.

It's only when someone has taken the time and trouble to read his books and then makes the connection between him and me—Davidson and his Rob—that the trouble begins.

It is there, you see, on the page, that the mistake occurs. We are constantly mistaken for each other. His readers (you happy few!), especially those who know me, Rob, sometimes mistakenly think that they see me on the page, in some incident or action, some image or quip of dialogue. But they are never correct. Davidson has fooled them because he is a thief. He steals unmercifully, without conscience or compunction, from those closest to him and from the world at large.

Mostly, he steals from me. From my memory.

You'd think I would resent that. I probably should. For when he steals a memory he doesn't simply take it verbatim. Invariably, he changes it. Paints the red barn blue. He makes me taller, smarter, quicker than I am. Or dumber, uglier, Republican. Or he puts me in Phoenix when I was really in Houston. He makes me older or younger, changes my name, my sex, my occupation.

As I say, I should probably resent that. But I do not. Far from it. For it is precisely *then*, when he's changed me so much that I cannot recognize myself, that I see myself most clearly. And I love him for that. That is why I work unstintingly for him, making sure that his two hours are given freely and are taken without interruption or distraction.

It is not that Davidson cannot exist without his Rob, but that there is no Rob without his Davidson. There is no reality that is not finally mediated by an elaborate fantasy.